Anonymous

Lottie and Grace or the Two Paths - A Tale

Anonymous

Lottie and Grace or the Two Paths - A Tale

ISBN/EAN: 9783337030445

Printed in Europe, USA, Canada, Australia, Japan

Cover: Foto ©Andreas Hilbeck / pixelio.de

More available books at **www.hansebooks.com**

LOTTIE.

LOTTIE AND GRACE;

OR,

THE TWO PATHS.

𝔄 𝔗𝔞𝔩𝔢.

BY THE AUTHOR OF

'AUNT ANNIE'S STORIES,' 'BROTHER BERTIE,'

ETC. ETC.

𝔚𝔦𝔱𝔥 𝔍𝔩𝔩𝔲𝔰𝔱𝔯𝔞𝔱𝔦𝔬𝔫𝔰.

SEELEY, JACKSON, AND HALLIDAY, 54 FLEET STREET.
LONDON. MDCCCLXIX.

LOTTIE AND GRACE, OR THE TWO PATHS.

'Charity envieth not ; charity vaunteth not itself; is not puffed up.'

It was the close of a warm day in spring, little
Lottie Allen had been enjoying a long walk with
some little friends on Hampstead Heath, just then
looking very pretty with its fresh green tints,

and snowy-looking bushes of hawthorn. Lottie
thought it the most lovely place in the world, and
no wonder, for it was the most like country that
she had ever seen, shut up as she generally was in
their home in one of the dullest, most cheerless
parts of London.

How she wished her mother could enjoy it with her, but that was out of the question. Mrs. Allen could never walk far, and when she came home from her daily work of teaching four little children who lived in a neighbouring square, she was generally too tired to care to go out again. And in the evening she taught Lottie, so that there really was very little time to spare for merrymaking.

Lottie knew this quite well, but still she could not feel quite contented when she thought how pale her mother often looked, and how much good it would do her, if she too could go for long walks into the country and breathe the fresh pure air. Every year Lottie lived this feeling grew stronger ; it is true she was too young when her father died to miss the comforts and pleasures that had gone with him, but she was not at all too young to see that many people who apparently did not want it half so much had plenty of money ; and it must be confessed she often wished that such people would bestow part of their superabundant wealth on her mother, who wanted it so very much.

Many such thoughts as this passed through Lottie's busy little brain as she trudged homeward; she was a sensible, observant child, and she had noticed for some days past that her mother had grown paler and paler, and that when she came home just before tea she often seemed quite worn out. Lottie wondered whether her mother was really worse than she said she was, and by the time she reached home, she had almost made up her mind to ask Mrs. Brand, the lady that lived in the drawing-room, what she thought about the matter.

But she was spared the trouble, for when she had reached her home, kissed her mother, taken off her things and sat down to tea, Mrs. Allen began: 'Do you know, Lottie, where I went on my way home?'

'No, mamma; oh, do tell me, have you been for a nice walk?'

'Not much of a walk, that's no treat to me, Lottie,' replied her mother, with a sad smile; 'no, I went to see our old friend, Mr. Darnell.'

'The doctor!' said Lottie, dropping her tea-spoon in dismay; 'oh, mother, are you going to be very ill?'

'I hope not,' replied Mrs. Allen, laughing at her terror; 'I only went to him to ask him if he

couldn't give me something to make me stronger.
I am not very strong; am I, Lottie?'

'No, indeed, mamma, you're dreadfully weak,
I think; but are you sure you are not going to be
ill? I should be so dreadfully frightened.'

'I should think you would, you poor little
mite,' said Mrs. Allen, stroking her head fondly;
'but when I have taken that great bottle of medicine, I hope I shall be very strong once more.'

Lottie looked greatly relieved; but as she
watched her mother's languid movements, and
noticed even more than she had before how thin
and pale she was, she began to think that the
medicine must be wonderful stuff indeed, if it
could make her thoroughly strong again.

'Didn't Mr. Darnell say anything else, mamma?'
she inquired at length; 'didn't he say that you
oughtn't to do so much?'

'It is easy for people to say that, Lottie,'
replied Mrs. Allen, half sadly; 'but you know, if
I sit with my hands before me all day, there will
be no money to buy food, and that is not likely
to make me any stronger.'

Lottie mused over these words, then suddenly
she exclaimed, 'Mamma, wouldn't it do you ever

so much good to go to the sea-side just now? Sophy's mamma is going because she is not very strong, and I think it would do you so much good.'

Mrs. Allen laughed.

' Why, Lottie, what are you thinking of, child?' she said; 'where's the money to come from? Don't you know it costs a great deal of money to go to the sea?'

' Does it, mamma? I think everything costs a great deal of money,' said poor Lottie, sadly; 'and money does go so fast. But didn't Mr. Darnell say the sea would do you good?'

' Yes, he said so, but of course he knew I couldn't go,' replied Mrs. Allen. 'Lottie, my child, don't begin longing for what can't be.'

Poor little Lottie said no more; but though she tried very hard indeed, she could not leave off thinking about the sea, and wishing,—oh, so much,—that some good fairy would give her mother the money to go. At first it was only on her mother's account that she longed to be able to go, but before long she found herself trying to imagine what the sea was like, and picturing herself running about on the beach, watching the great waves

of which her mother had often told her; for Lottie
had never seen the sea, and had but a faint idea
of what it was like.

How long these thoughts kept her awake that
night, I am sure I cannot tell you, but when she
went to sleep, it was only to dream about the
delights and wonders of the sea; and when she
woke up the next morning, the bright pictures
her imagination had formed were still present to
her mind.

Her mother thought she must have forgotten
all about her little schemes, and began to wonder
what she was dreaming about, when she noticed
that instead of chattering all breakfast-time as
she usually did, Lottie seemed lost in thought, or
up in the clouds, as she would herself have
called it.

She was just going to inquire what her little
daughter was thinking about, when her thoughts
were turned in another direction by the sound of
the postman's knock. Since her husband's death,
and all the troubles that followed that event, this
interesting person had been by no means such a
frequent visitor as in the days of her prosperity.
His knock was always a welcome sound to little

Lottie; and as she ran to take the letter on this particular morning, she had a kind of lingering idea that it might contain the money to take her mother to the sea.

But when the letter was opened, and no bank-note dropped out, Lottie's bright hopes sank again. It was from her uncle, her father's brother, whom Lottie had never seen, for he lived at a place a long way off in the north of England. All she knew about him was that he had a wife and a number of little children, one of whom Grace, her mother had told her, was about her own age. He was very rich too, Lottie remembered; and as she watched her mother reading the letter, she began to wonder if he was to be the good fairy of her waking dreams. Perhaps he had somehow heard that her mother was ill, and had written this letter to invite her to go and stay at his beautiful house in the country.

'Wouldn't you like to see your cousin Grace, Lottie?' inquired Mrs. Allen, as she folded up the letter and put it in her pocket; 'she is just your age, and a very nice little girl, I believe.'

'Oh, mamma, are we to go then?' exclaimed Lottie, eagerly jumping to the rapid conclusion

that her wish was about to be fulfilled. 'I am
so glad, I am sure it will make you well.'

'Gently,' said Mrs. Allen, smiling; 'you are
in too great a hurry, Lottie; I never said we
were going anywhere, did I? It is your uncle
and aunt and cousins who are coming to London.
Your uncle writes to tell me so, and he kindly
says that he hopes you and Grace will become
good friends.'

Poor Lottie looked bitterly disappointed; but
she tried to get the better of her vexation, and
inquired when they were coming.

'In less than a week,' Mrs. Allen replied; and
then she remembered that she had spent more
time than usual that morning at the breakfast-
table, and rose hastily to prepare for her daily
duties.

How terribly long the hours of that day
seemed to Lottie! When her mother was gone
she fetched her lesson-books and set to work as
usual to learn the lessons she had to say to her
mother in the evening. She wrote her copy, and
did her sum, and then she began to learn her
hymn. It was a very easy one, and an especial
favourite of Lottie's; and yet, very strangely, it

seemed determined not to be conquered. Lottie
thought she would rest awhile, and so she got
her work, and having looked to see how much
her mother had pinned for her to sew, she threaded
her needle and set to work.

But, before long, the work went down on
her knee, and the needle was left sticking out,
while, with her head resting on her hand,
Lottie's thoughts went wandering off to her
uncle's letter.

She wondered what he was like, and whether
he knew how poor they were. Surely if he did
he would have helped them long ago, since he
had got such a lot of money. It must be so nice,
Lottie thought, to help people who wanted all
sorts of things they could not get; and then she
began to wish she had a fine house, and plenty
of money to give to all the beggars she met in
the street.

How long she would have continued her idle
musing it is hard to say, if she had not been
interrupted by the voice of the lady who lived
in the drawing-room calling her by name from
the top of the stairs. She was going out a little
way, she said, and if Lottie liked she might go

with her. Lottie hesitated, remembering her un-
finished lessons ; but she knew that her mother
liked her to go out with Mrs. Brand, who was
a kind motherly woman, and took good care of
her ; so she hastily put the books away in the
cupboard, and ran to get ready.

The days and weeks of Lottie's life had so
little change that they passed away very rapidly.
The day came for her first visit to her cousins
almost before she had time to think about it ;
which perhaps was rather a good thing, for Lottie
was shy, and by no means fond of making new
acquaintances. It would take a long time to tell
you all that happened on that wonderful day, the
first day in her life that Lottie Allen had spent
altogether away from her own little home ; as she
herself said to her mother on her return, it seemed
more like a week than only a day.

Mrs. Allen laughed, and said she thought if
that was the case, she must be very tired and had ·
better make haste and go to bed.

'Oh, no, please, mamma, do let me stay up
a little while,' pleaded Lottie, earnestly ; 'it is
the best part of it all to be able to tell you
about it.'

'Well, go on then,' said Mrs. Allen; 'what

did you do when the big carriage had taken you

to Uncle George's house, did Grace meet you at the door ?'

'Oh, yes, mamma, Grace and Georgie, and Freddy and Minnie too. Oh, Minnie is such a funny little thing, and so is Freddy, but I like Freddy best. He has got such a big dog, mamma, and he and Minnie dress it up like a Turk, with a turban on, and a feather brush to do instead of a plume. The dog's name is Turk, and he is such a good old fellow, he lets them do just what they like to him. Then, mamma, we had tea in the garden; there is such a big garden behind the house, and Grace showed me all her dolls; she has got nine dolls of her own, and Minnie has six : they are such beauties, mamma,—oh, I should like you to see them so much !'

'Perhaps I may have the pleasure of making their acquaintance some day, Lottie,' replied Mrs. Allen, smiling at her little daughter's eagerness; 'but you have not told me yet how you like Grace ?'

Lottie hesitated, coloured, and looked rather uncomfortable, at last she said : 'I liked her very much indeed at first, mamma; she was so kind, and seemed so pleased when I liked anything, but in the afternoon I didn't like her half so much, she was so cross to Georgie, she would not play at any game he liked, and she called Minnie a stupid little thing.'

'That was not very nice, certainly,' replied Mrs. Allen, 'but it was a very hot day, perhaps Gracie was tired.'

'Well,' said Lottie, growing more bold as she went on, 'I didn't like her at all this evening, she talks so much about her papa being so rich, and about all the new dresses she has; I think, if all that's true, he might give you some of his money, mamma.'

'Hush! hush!' said her mother, 'we must not envy your cousins their nice things; have you forgotten what you learnt last Sunday, "Charity envieth not," and all we said about it, Lottie?'

'No, mamma,' said the child, somewhat ashamed; 'but if they've got so much, it wouldn't hurt them much to give you just enough to go to the sea-side.'

Mrs. Allen shook her head.

'You forget, Lottie,' she said, 'that your Uncle George has got five children to bring up, and I have only one, he *wants* a great deal more money than I do.'

Lottie was silent ; she had not thought of this side of the question, and though she could not help fancying that her uncle had a great deal more than five times as much money as her mother, she was not fond enough of arithmetic to enter very earnestly into the calculation. She had found out that Grace had a great deal more pocket-money than she ever dreamed of possessing ; and though she did not care to own it even to herself, that discovery had not increased her affectionate feelings towards her cousin. Ah, Lottie, take care, envy and dislike always go hand in hand.

Some days passed, during which Lottie saw nothing of her cousins ; but she had not got tired of talking of her visit to them when a letter came from her aunt, begging that her mamma would let her go the next day with her cousins to visit the Zoological Gardens. Lottie jumped about with delight at the news, and could hardly be brought sufficiently to her senses to eat her breakfast as usual. It is true she had been to the Zoological Gardens before, but that was years and years ago, Lottie said, and she had forgotten all about it.

Mrs. Allen began to consider, and found out that the 'years and years' could not possibly be more than three, and she said that she was sorry to find Lottie had such a bad memory. However, during the solitary day that followed the invitation, Lottie found time to remember many things that had happened on her former visit, and her lessons with her mother in the evening were constantly interrupted by such exclamations as these, 'Oh, mamma, do you remember how we fed the polar bear?' or, 'Do you think we shall see the lions fed, mamma, I hope we shall, don't you?' and various other remarks which were certainly not to be found in her lesson-books.

At first Mrs. Allen only smiled at these observations, and excused her inattention, remembering how seldom Lottie had a holiday or treat of any kind; but when it began to grow late, and still two lessons remained to be done, she said, gravely, 'Lottie, you really must not chatter any more, I am very tired to-night, so make haste and finish your lessons.'

Lottie looked up anxiously. 'Oh, mamma, you are not going to be ill, are you?' she inquired eagerly; for she felt that a good deal depended on the answer.

'I don't know, Lottie; I hope not. I think I have a little cold; my throat is sore, and I am shaking and shivering all over. We will go to bed early to-night.'

A great cloud seemed all at once to come over Lottie's spirits, rising just before so much beyond their usual pitch. She bent her head over her slate, and a great tear fell, half blotting out the sum she was doing. Hastily she wiped it off, lest her mother should see it, and then set to work as hard as possible to get her lessons finished, that they might go to bed.

Bed, in Lottie's opinion, was the best remedy for all complaints, and she tried to believe that if she had a good long night's rest, her mother would wake up nearly as well as usual. But she had strange misgivings, which kept her awake what seemed to her an immense time after she got into bed. She had heard it said that her father's last illness began with a cold, and that at first everybody thought it was not of much consequence. Perhaps her mother was worse than she thought, and if she was not better to-morrow, Lottie felt sure she must not go to the Zoological Gardens. If *she* were ill, she knew her mother would never leave her merely for her own pleasure, and poor little Lottie tried hard to make up her mind not to be very unhappy if the next morning she found she could not go.

Still it did seem very hard, it was so seldom she had any treats, and if her mother was going to be ill, why need it be on the very day when she was going out? You see Lottie had not yet fully learnt that there is One who settles even these little things for us, and that when we make our arrangements for the future, we should think to ourselves, I will do this, or that, if God pleases, but if He has settled it differently for me, why His way must be best, because He knows much better than I do all that is going to happen.

You will not be very much surprised to hear that Lottie woke very early the next morning. Her first thought was her mother, and seeing she was not asleep, with a fast-beating heart, and very anxious tone of voice, she inquired, 'Mamma, have you had a good night?'

'I have hardly slept at all, darling,' said Mrs.
Allen, speaking with difficulty, 'my throat was so
sore I could scarcely breathe. I think I must stay
in bed to breakfast. Do you think you can get
up now, dear, and make me a cup of tea as soon as
you are dressed? Perhaps I shall feel better when
I have had something to drink.'

Lottie jumped up quickly and began to dress.
A great lump came into her throat, and prevented
her speaking. She had never seen her mother
look so ill, and even the Zoological Gardens were
forgotten in the dread that oppressed her that this
cold might be the beginning of something worse.

The cup of tea was soon made, for Mrs. Brand
was always up early, and willingly supplied Lottie
with boiling water, telling her not to keep her
mother waiting till their own fire had burnt up.

Lottie carried the tea very carefully to her
mother, and then took her a nice little piece of
toast that kind Mrs. Brand had made for her; but
it was with great difficulty that Mrs. Allen could
swallow anything solid, and it was with a sad
heart and tearful eyes that poor Lottie returned to
her neighbour's room to eat her breakfast there.

Mrs. Brand had heard of Lottie's intended visit

to the Zoological Gardens, and when she saw her
tears, she naturally enough imagined that they
were caused by a fear that she would not be able
to go with her cousins. So thinking to console
her, the kind woman said in her motherly way,
'Now don't be fretting about your treat, I'll see
that your mother does not want for anything,
and you can go the same as if nothing was the
matter.'

'Oh, Mrs. Brand, it isn't that,' sobbed Lottie;
'I would not cry about that, but don't you think
mamma's very ill indeed, don't you think she's
going to be ill like papa was?'

'Ill like your papa was, why that was rapid
consumption! No, I don't think anything of the
sort; it's a bad cold, my dear, nothing worse.
And as to your holiday, I'm sure she wouldn't
have you stay at home for anything.'

'I couldn't go, I should be so unhappy,' replied
the child, only half comforted; 'but I wish you'd
come and see her, Mrs. Brand, I'm sure she's very
bad, she can hardly breathe.'

Mrs. Brand was very willing, and at once
decided that a mustard-plaster, a good strong one,
was just the thing to set her throat right. So she

made it and put it on, and soon after it had been taken off, the poor invalid fell asleep.

Before she woke up, Lottie's cousins arrived to fetch her, but in spite of their remonstrances and Mrs. Brand's assurances that she might just as well go, the child continued firm in her resolve to stay at home with her mother.

'Mamma wouldn't have left me if I'd been ill,' she persisted, and at last the carriage drove off, her cousins declaring it was a great shame, and that they did not care a bit about going, now that Lottie was not with them.

'Well,' exclaimed Mrs. Brand, when Lottie came up to her room soon after to fetch something she wanted, 'you are a good, self-denying little thing, I will say that for you.'

'Self-denying, Mrs. Brand,' replied Lottie, opening her large blue eyes very wide; 'why? oh! because I stayed at home with mamma?'

'Yes, to be sure, it isn't often you get a holiday, and it does seem a shame you should be done out of this, after looking forward to it all yesterday too.'

Lottie stood considering a minute, then she said, 'But, Mrs. Brand, it isn't self-denial, because

I didn't want to go, at least not with my whole heart, because, if I had gone, I should have been thinking about mamma all the time, and then it wouldn't have been any pleasure.'

'Wouldn't it? well, you are a queer child,' said her kind friend, 'most children would have gone, and never given their mothers another thought till they saw them again.'

'Oh, Mrs. Brand,' said Lottie, indignantly, 'that must be when their mothers don't care for them, and my mamma does care for me; why, if she hadn't got me, I daresay she needn't go out to teach every day.'

'Perhaps not, and then she wouldn't have got ill,' continued Mrs. Brand; 'she got wet through last night coming home, I know, for I met her at the door, and the rain was pouring down in buckets full.'

'I must go and put the parlour to rights,' said little Lottie, 'while mother's asleep; perhaps she'll like me to read to her when she awakes. Please, Mrs. Brand, if she doesn't seem better when she wakes, do you think I'd better go and fetch the doctor?'

'She'll be better when she wakes, child; don't

you be fidgeting about her ; and as for the doctor,
we'll try and do without him, if we can.'

Lottie tried to feel more cheerful, but it was
hard ; she had had a harder fight with herself
about giving up the Zoological Gardens than she
chose to admit, and though cheery Mrs. Brand
told her there was nothing to be anxious about,
she could not feel so confident.

However, she ran downstairs on tiptoe, dusted
the sitting-room as quietly as possible, and then
took some of her lesson-books into the bed-room
that she might have something to do till her
mother should wake.

Contrary to Mrs. Brand's prediction; Mrs.
Allen did not seem any better when she woke.
She said her head ached terribly, and her chest
was so sore she could scarcely breathe. Poor
Lottie was sadly frightened to see how she
coughed whenever she tried to speak, and in great
alarm begged her mother to let her put on her
hat, and run and fetch their old friend, Mr.
Darnell.

But Mrs. Allen would not hear of such a
thing ; her cold would soon be better, she said, if
only she could get some ease from the headache

that prevented her from sleeping quietly; and then she remembered that Lottie ought to have started some time before with her cousins. She inquired anxiously whether they had not sent for her, and was very sorry when she found that the child had refused to go on her account. But Lottie thought that the fond, loving look which her mother gave her, when she found what she had done, was quite reward enough for the little sacrifice. If only her mother would get well, she thought, she should never be unhappy again; but at present this happiness was not in store for little Lottie. A basin of broth that Mrs. Brand had declared would do wonders, it was so beautifully strong and good, failed to produce the marvellous effect that little Lottie longed to see. She thought as she carried it without spilling a drop to her mother, that she would be sure to feel better after she had drunk it, and if she went to sleep then, she would be sure to wake up better. In spite of all her protestations, sleep when at last it came did not make Mrs. Allen well, and the next day even cheery Mrs. Brand suggested that it was time to send for the doctor.

So the doctor came with a very grave face, and

he shook his head so many times while question-
ing her mother, that poor Lottie began to think
that she must be very bad indeed. But some
doctors have a habit of shaking their heads, and
Mr. Darnell was one of these men. Those that
knew him best did not augur anything very
dreadful from this habit, they knew it was merely
meant to express sympathy, and when his grey
head wagged faster than usual, they understood
quite well that he merely meant to say, 'I know
quite well all you feel, you need not trouble
yourself to tell me,' and so the more he shook his
head, the wiser people thought him.

But when the old doctor perceived how frightened poor little Lottie was, he did his best to
comfort her. 'Your mother will soon get over
this little attack, my little woman,' he said, kindly,
'and then we must try and make her stronger,
so that a little rain won't give her such a bad
cold again;' and so saying, he bustled away.
Lottie dried her eyes, and tried to look bright
and cheerful, that her mother might not be
anxious, and then, like an affectionate child as
she was, she set to work to make her mother as
comfortable as possible.

The days passed slowly by; they seldom go very fast in a sick room, and Mrs. Allen gradually got better. Lottie was very much delighted one day to hear her say that she had scarcely any pain now in her chest, except when she coughed; unfortunately that happened rather too often. And again Mr. Darnell began to talk of her going to some warm place by the sea-side, till Lottie felt as if she would do anything if only her mother could manage it. But the old difficulty still remained, where was the money to come from? In fact, her mother's illness had made this difficulty greater than ever, and though Lottie longed and longed, she was obliged to admit that it was quite impossible.

Once or twice the idea had occurred to her that her uncle would lend them the money if they asked, and in her eagerness to find some way out of the difficulty, she ventured to propose the scheme to her mother. But Mrs. Allen would not consent to any such plan; she would not run into debt as long as she could help it, she said, and certainly not on her own account. So Lottie tried to think of some other plan.

Such was the state of things one evening,

when Lottie returned home from spending the afternoon with her cousins. Her mother was quite able to sit up now, and as kind Mrs. Brand was always willing to do anything for her that she could not do for herself, she would not consent to the child's staying at home on her account.

It was a great relief to Lottie to feel the great weight of pressing anxiety lifted off her spirits, and to mix again with children of her own age. Her mother knew she needed the change, and looked forward with pleasure to seeing her return in the evening full of life and gaiety as of old.

And the little face certainly did look less oppressed with care and anxiety than it had lately done, when the child came bounding in, eager to tell all that had happened to her during the day, yet quiet and watchful lest by her long stories she should tire the invalid. But Mrs. Allen was quite equal to hearing of the feats of Turk, the funny little sayings of Freddy, and of the two new dolls that had been added to Grace's family since she saw her last. But the mention of these two dolls brought a thoughtful look over Lottie's face, which her mother noticed, saying, ' I hope, Lottie, you are not wishing you had got some of your cousin's beautiful dolls and playthings, or envying her her nice large house, and lots of pocket-money ?'

'Oh, no, mamma,' replied the child, 'I don't want the dolls, but I do wish very much I had some of the money my cousins spend on their toys, because then we could go to the sea, and you would get quite well and strong.'

Mrs. Allen smiled.

'Still the same dream, my child ; can't you think of something else to wish for, Lottie, for certainly there is no chance of your obtaining your wish in this respect. But I hope you did not tell any one your thoughts, it would look like asking for the money.'

Lottie coloured.

'I did just tell Gracie what I wished, mamma ; I did not know there was any harm in it,' she replied, timidly.

Mrs. Allen looked vexed, but she said nothing, and Lottie continued,—

'Mamma, did uncle ever give you any money in his life ?'

'No, Lottie ; I never asked for it, or I daresay he would have done so. Very likely he

gives all he can spare to people poorer than we
are.'

Lottie thought a minute, and then said, ' Yes,
I remember now, I saw aunt give some money, I
think it was sixpence,
to a poor ragged boy
in the streets, and he
did look so pleased,
mamma.'

' Very likely he wanted the money badly
enough,' said Mrs. Allen ; ' but now it is time
you went. Just take this large pair of scissors
back to Mrs. Brand, she lent them me this after-

noon, and then see how quickly you can get to bed.'

Lottie obeyed. She was fast enough getting undressed when she once began the operation, but being somewhat fond of a gossip, she stayed talking to their goodnatured neighbour some time before she went to her own room.

A few days after the above conversation, Lottie's uncle and aunt, with her cousin Grace, called to say good-bye, as they were about to return to their home in the north of England. Lottie was very sorry to think she should not see her cousin again, perhaps for a very long time, but she was so disappointed to think that her uncle was really going away without doing anything for them, that she could hardly think of anything else. She had often read in story-books of little girls who, like her, had set their hearts on something quite beyond their reach, when a good fairy appeared and set matters right. Her uncle, she had flattered herself, would prove their good fairy, rather a substantial one it is true; but this hope seemed destined to be disappointed, and poor Lottie's face was very gloomy indeed, when she returned to her mother's room, after seeing them take their departure.

Mrs. Allen not having indulged in such large
expectations, smiled at her woe-begone face, and
tried to cheer her by admiring some little parting
gifts which her uncle had given her ; but Lottie
hardly answered her, and very soon escaped to her
friend Mrs. Brand, who was always more ready to
listen to her complaints of her rich relations, than
her mother was.

The kind-hearted woman sympathised warmly
with Lottie's disappointment, she had often noticed, she said, 'that rich relations didn't do much
for their poor friends, and she often wondered
what use they were : she had none, and she was
often glad of it, for if they did anything for you,
they expected such an amount of gratitude in
return, that she would rather by half do without
their kindness.'

Lottie did not quite agree with her in all she
said, for she had passed some very happy days
with her cousins, and received some very welcome
presents from her uncle and aunt, neither of which
pleasures she could despise, nor say she would
rather have been without them. But this did not
prevent her being very much comforted by Mrs.
Brand's remarks. She went to bed at last, half
believing that she and her mother had a sort of

right to some of her uncle's property and money, and almost convinced that they had been decidedly ill used, because he had gone away without making them as rich as himself.

But the conversation she had had with little Lottie had left Mrs. Brand very uncomfortable. She and her husband had long been saving up their spare money to enable them to go with their two little ones to the sea-side; more than two years they had promised themselves this treat, and this year they fully intended to carry out the plan. Now Mrs. Brand was strong and well, and as she listened to the tale of little Lottie's fears for her mother, she had asked herself if it was not very selfish of her to think of such a treat, when there was some one living so near who needed it so much more. A long time she debated the matter in her own mind, but she could see no way out of the difficulty. If it were only herself, she thought she could easily give up the plan and send the widow and her child instead. But the kind-hearted, unselfish woman had her husband and children to consider, and however ready she might be to deny herself for the widow and fatherless, she knew that they wanted the change sorely.

She smiled to think of her little ones' delight at seeing the sea and playing on the sands, and of her husband's pale, thin face, growing brown and healthy-looking in the bracing sea air; and as she sat by her window that long summer evening turning over these things in her mind, she said to herself that it was impossible she could do anything for the poor woman; John must have the holiday he had worked so hard for, and she determined that she would say nothing to him about the poor woman, that he might not be troubled about her.

But it was seldom that good Mrs. Brand kept such a resolution as this, nor did she succeed in doing so on the present occasion. Very few questions on her husband's part, served to draw the whole story of her perplexity from her, and when she wound up the account by saying—'Of course it's of no use, we can't afford to help her;' she looked anxiously into his face to see if he agreed with her. But he was a man of very few words, and after listening attentively to her story and asking one or two questions about the widow's state, he made no further remark on the subject that night.

'He thinks there's nothing to be done,' said the wife to herself, 'what will pay for four won't pay for six ; there can't be any doubt about that. I wish I hadn't said anything about it.' Then she said to herself, that if she did not want the change, there could be no doubt her husband did, for had he not been growing paler and paler ever since she married him, and all from nothing but hard work and constant confinement in a close office, with no change from one year's end to another.

Her children too, every one said sea air would do them so much good ; the elder one, Annie, was certainly as well as a child could be, but Alice, the little one, her mother's darling, had been ailing for some time. It was hard to say what was the matter with her, for she seldom complained of any pain, but she was often hot, and feverish, and restless at night. The mother often felt anxious about her, and she had reckoned on this visit to the sea-side doing her so much good ; 'You see if we don't bring her back looking quite different,' she had said to her husband only the night before, and now as she recalled her anxieties for her cherished little one,

she said that after all she was not so selfish as
she had thought at first, for it really was not
for herself that she cared about the excursion, but
simply and solely for her husband and children.

And while she was turning these things over
in her mind, a sound of distant crying from the
room where the two children slept, recalled all her
anxious cares for her little sickly one ; some bad
dreams had no doubt disturbed her in her sleep ;
and the mother hastened to go and comfort her.
The child was sitting up in bed, her little face
crimson with terror, and her eyes gazing wildly
around her. But the appearance of her mother
reassured her, and Annie, the elder one, who
had been awakened by her cries, at once composed
herself to sleep again, murmuring, 'Mother's here,
it's all right, go to sleep, Alie.'

But Alice was too wide awake to follow this
advice, she clung to her mother, shaking and
trembling with affright, and could only say, 'Oh,
mother, hold me tight, tight.' Mrs. Brand sat
down by the bed, and took the little one in her
arms, and very soon Alice was able to tell her how
when she was asleep she had got down, down, far
under the clothes, and dreamed she was falling

ALICE'S DREAM.

into a river, till she woke, and it was so dreadful, she thought she never should get out.

Her mother comforted her, and before long Alice was quieted and fast asleep again in her little bed; the red flush gone from her face, and no signs remaining of her fright, save that now and then a deep sigh escaped from between the little rosy lips, and her little hand still clutched a corner of the bed-clothes so firmly, that her mother did not attempt to disengage it, for fear of waking her.

Now the great news of the intended holiday had hitherto been kept a secret from Annie and Alice, for fear, as Mrs. Brand said, that anything might happen to hinder it; she did not like children to be disappointed. But now the day was so near, that there was no need to keep it a secret any longer; so it was settled that their father should tell them the next morning while they were having their breakfast. Annie and Alice were so well brought up, that there was no fear of their joy being so uproarious as to endanger the cups and saucers, or even to take away their appetites. In fact, their mother had trained them to sit as quiet at meals as if they were two little

old women, so breakfast or tea-time was always
the time chosen for telling the little ones any
specially good piece of news.

I am afraid Lottie would hardly have been so
quiet if such news had been told to her; but then
it was not her nature to sit still when she was
pleased, she liked to jump about and sing, and
Mrs. Brand said it was not to be wondered at, as
she had so few treats or pleasures.

But when Annie and Alice heard their father
say, 'Children, I have got some good news to tell
you;' they did not scream out or clap their hands,
or do anything noisy or troublesome. No, they
sat quite still, and did not say a word. Annie
laid her spoon down again, she had taken it up to
begin her bread-and-milk, and little Alice smoothed
her pinafore over her knees, and folded her arms as
she did in the church when the clergyman began
his sermon. Then seeing they were attentive,
Mr. Brand resumed, 'Children, we are going to
the sea-side, to see that great and wonderful sea
that your mother has told you about, you must
try and be good and give your mother as little
trouble as possible; it is a treat you will not have
many times in your life.'

Then Annie thought she ought to say something, but she couldn't think of anything at all to
say, except 'Yes, father,' and she felt sure that
was not the right thing at all, and was very glad
indeed when her mother said, 'Children, eat
your breakfasts, and don't talk, your father and I
have plenty to think about.'

Now, though Annie and Alice were such quiet,
well-behaved little girls, they dearly loved to talk
to each other; and as they mightn't talk at breakfast time, they made haste to finish, that they
might run away to their own little room and
chatter to their hearts' content.

Meanwhile, their father and mother were
discussing a little idea that had come into Mr.
Brand's head during the night. What this idea
was, I think you will guess, when I tell you that
soon after her husband went out, Mrs. Brand paid
a visit to Mrs. Allen in her room and had a long
talk with her; and in the evening, to her great
delight, Lottie heard that it was settled that she
and her mother were to go with the Brands to
Margate on the following Saturday.

At first she was too wild with delight to think
about anything but the anticipated pleasure, but

by the next morning she had calmed down a little,
and when she was seated by her mother's side hard
at work mending an old print frock, which Mrs.
Allen had decided would be quite good enough to
wear on the beach, she began her questions :

'Mamma, have you got any more money
lately ?'

'Only what I had kept to pay the doctor's bill,
Lottie,' said her mamma ; 'didn't I tell you last
night that Mr. Darnell would not take a far-
thing ?'

'Oh, mamma, how kind of him,' exclaimed
Lottie ; 'and will that be enough to pay for our
going to Margate ?'

'I am afraid not,' said Mrs. Allen, sighing. 'I
hardly know whether I ought to do it ; but Mrs.
Brand was so eager, I hardly know how to refuse.
She said I was to pay what I could and they
would lend the rest. I don't believe they mean to
let me pay it back again, but I shall try. And I
am afraid they are going for a shorter time than
they had intended just in order to take us with
them.'

Lottie looked very thoughtful ; at last she
said :

'Mother, I don't like their doing that, but I am sure they would be really sorry if we didn't go. Don't you remember how often Mrs. Brand says, "It is more blessed to give than to receive."'

'Yes, I know,' said Mrs. Allen, 'I can't deprive her of this pleasure, and yet I hardly know if I ought to run into debt.'

'Run into debt,' said a cheery voice at the door, and Mrs. Brand came in, 'there's no need. You told me you could manage the journey-money, and when you get down there, why, all we ask is that you will be our visitors; and I'm such an old friend now that I shall be offended if you don't let me have the pleasure of doing you a good turn when it's in my power,—I shall indeed,' added the good-natured woman.

Mrs. Allen smiled, and said, 'If that's the case, I suppose I must say yes, with many, many thanks.'

'Say "yes," that's right, but as for the thanks, why it's I that ought to say thank you; I've wanted you to go more than I can tell, and I shouldn't really enjoy it a bit if you were to stay at home. So the benefit's mine, you see.'

Mrs. Allen shook her head, with a smile, and then the two mothers began to discuss the preparations necessary for the trip. Lottie's, Annie's, and Alice's frocks were all examined, and the next two days were busy ones indeed ; there was so much to mend, so much to pack, so much bustle and running up and down stairs, that the three little girls thought they should never be ready in time.

However, as it was not Mrs. Brand's habit to rest or be quiet till things were done, she laboured on without ceasing till everything was completed, and by tea-time on Friday night the boxes were packed and everything was ready.

Little Alice innocently suggested that as they were quite ready they might as well set off at once. But this remark was considered very childish by Annie, who being two years older, and very nearly seven, knew a greal deal more about the ways of the world, and instantly replied that father had ordered the steamboat to be ready on Saturday, and so of course they could not go before.

This reasoning was quite convincing, and Alice immediately remembered that she wanted to know

a great many things about the steamboat, which
Annie or Lottie could doubtless tell her. All the
little girls had been in a train, so a journey by sea
was considered much more exciting and delightful.
But, unfortunately, Annie had never seen a steamboat, and could give her little sister very little
information on the subject. Lottie had seen these
wonderful contrivances once, when she went with
her mother over Waterloo Bridge ; but Mrs. Brand
said that the steamers that went to Margate were
bigger than those she had seen, so there was
nothing for it but to wait till Saturday, when
they would be able to find out all they wanted
to know.

Saturday came very soon, for though on
Friday night the little girls thought they had a
very long time to wait, after they had gone to
bed the hours flew very fast indeed, and in less
than no time, so it seemed to them, the morning
came, and the time to start.

All the little people were awake very early,
but not so early as bustling Mrs. Brand ; for
though everything seemed to be ready the night
before, she had many little things left to do.
Sandwiches could not be cut the night before,

and the good woman was determined that nobody
should be starved on the way. So she prepared
such a pile that the two little ones opened their
eyes very wide, and wondered who would be able
to eat all that basketful.

Their mother told them they would soon find
out that sea air made people hungry; and she
should be very much surprised if there were
any provisions left when they reached their
journey's end. This made little Alice look very
grave, and she inquired anxiously whether there
were any shops at Margate where they could get
any more, as she evidently did not approve of
the idea of fasting for such a length of time.

This inquiry made Mrs. Brand laugh so much
that Alice feared she had said something very
silly, and grew very red indeed when she heard
her mother tell Mrs. Allen what she had said,
adding, ' Only think of the children fancying they
were going to be taken to live in a desert, poor
little mites.' She thought they must think her
so very foolish, and she wished very much that
she could be as wise as her sister Annie, who
didn't always say the first thing that came into
her head.

However, even Annie talked a good deal of nonsense that morning, so excited was she at the thought of the journey, and Alice too could not quite keep her spirits within bounds.

Their quiet father was quite astonished at the noise they made, but kind Mrs. Brand only said, ' Never mind, father, they'll be quieter when they get on board the boat ; they can't help making a noise now, they never had such a treat in their lives.'

Then followed the delightful bustle of stowing the luggage and small people away in the cab, which as cabs are wont to be very unelastic things was no easy matter ; for five people, though three may not be very large, are quite enough to fill an ordinary-sized cab, and in this case there were a good many parcels to fill up the cracks.

However, where there's a will there's a way, and Mrs. Brand soon contrived to put everybody in but herself and Mr. Brand, who would of course go on the box with the driver ; then having made sure that nothing had been for-gotten, she made an attempt to squeeze herself in. It failed, and some baskets having been moved, she tried again with better success, seating herself apparently very comfortably in the corner by Mrs. Allen. Unfortunately the sandwich-basket had been placed in that corner, and neither basket nor sandwiches were any the better for having to bear the weight of Mrs. Brand's substantial figure. However, such little accidents as that are of small consequence to people who are determined to be happy, and the boat was reached in perfect safety and good-humour.

LONDON:

STRANGEWAYS AND WALDEN, Printers, Castle St. Leicester Sq.

WORKS BY THE SAME AUTHOR.

AUNT ANNIE'S STORIES ;

Or, The Birthdays at Gordon Manor. By the Author of 'True Stories for Little People.' In large 16mo. with Twelve Coloured, and Twenty Plain Illustrations, price 5s. cloth gilt. Each of the Stories may be had separately, bound in cloth, gilt, with Two Coloured and Three Plain Illustrations, price 1s.

1. LITTLE JOE AND HIS STRAWBERRY PLANT.
2. NORMAN AND ADA; OR, THE FIRST VISIT.
3. DONALD'S HAMPER.
4. THE BUNCH OF GRAPES.
5. LITTLE CHARLOTTE'S HOME IN BURMAH.
6. LITTLE NELLIE; OR, THE WAY TO BE HAPPY.

BROTHER BERTIE AND HIS FRIENDS IN THE FIELDS AND FLOWER-BEDS.

By the Author of 'Aunt Annie's Stories.'
In large 16mo. with Twelve Coloured, and Twenty-one Plain Illustrations, price 5s. cloth.

LITTLE FRIENDS IN THE VILLAGE.

A Story for Children. By the Author of 'Aunt Annie's Stories.'
In large 16mo. with Twenty-three Illustrations, 3s. 6d. cloth.

GREAT THINGS DONE BY LITTLE PEOPLE.

Large Type. Six Engravings. 2s. 6d.

WINGED THINGS.

True Stories about Birds. In 16mo. Twelve Engravings.
Large Type, 2s. 6d.

LITTLE ANIMALS DESCRIBED FOR LITTLE PEOPLE.

In 16mo. Large Type, Eight Engravings, 2s. 6d.

TRUE STORIES FOR LITTLE PEOPLE.

In 16mo. Large Type, with Ten Engravings, price 2s. 6d. cloth.

BOOKS FOR THE YOUNG.

WHAT MAKES ME GROW; or, Walks and Talks with Amy Dudley. By the Author of 'Harry Lawton's Adventures.' With Twelve Illustrations by FROLICH. Price 3s. 6d. cloth elegant.

LITTLE ROSY'S VOYAGE OF DISCOVERY, undertaken in Company with her Cousin Charley. In large 8vo. with Forty-eight Illustrations by L. FROLICH. Price 6s. 6d. cloth.

'How children will enjoy this book! It is a story so natural in its conception, and so naturally told, that children will not ask if it is true, but will deem it a veracious book of travels.'—*Standard.*

LITTLE ROSY'S TRAVELS; or, Country Scenes in the South of France. With Twenty-four Illustrations by L. FROLICH. Fourth Thousand, large 16mo. 6s. cloth.

'A thorough child's story, capitally told and beautifully illustrated.'—*Record.*

PETER LIPP; or, the Story of a Boy's Venture. Adapted from the French. Twenty-six Engravings on Wood. Crown 8vo. 5s. cloth.

'It is a simple tale, but its charm lies in the very pretty style in which it is told, and we may add, also, in the remarkable excellence of the illustrations with which it is plentifully adorned.'—*Guardian.*

THE STORY OF A ROUND LOAF. Thirty-two Designs by E. FROMENT. In small 4to. 3s. 6d. cloth.

'The skill of an accomplished artist is shown in these graceful playthings of art; they are admirably drawn, and display feeling and taste. The story is happily told, and a pleasant book has been made.'—*Art Journal.*

THE WARRINGTONS ABROAD; or, Twelve Months in Germany, Italy, and Egypt. Thirty-five Engravings, small 4to. 5s. cloth.

'A capital book, beautifully got up, and admirably illustrated. It is a marvel of cheapness, and yet will do credit to a drawing-room table.'—*John Bull.*

HARRY LAWTON'S ADVENTURES; or, a Young Sailor's Wanderings in Strange Lands. Thirty-six Engravings, small 4to. 5s. cloth.

'A most attractive volume for young people. Such books at such prices are among the marvels of literature '—*Record.*

THE WHALE'S STORY: Passages from the Life of a Leviathan. Large Type, with Six Engravings. 2s. 6d. cloth.

SEELEY, JACKSON, AND HALLIDAY, 54 FLEET STREET.